With special thanks to Natalie Doherty

For Louis x

Text Copyright © 2014 by Hothouse Fiction
Illustrations Copyright © 2014 by Sophy Williams

All rights reserved. Published by Scholastic Inc., 557 Broadway, New York, NY 10012, *Publishers since 1920*. SCHOLASTIC and associated logos are trademarks and/or registered trademarks of Scholastic Inc. Published by arrangement with Nosy Crow Ltd. Series created by Hothouse Fiction.

First published in the United Kingdom in 2014 by Nosy Crow Ltd., The Crow's Nest, 10a Lant St., London, SE1 1QR.

The publisher does not have any control over and does not assume any responsibility for author or third-party websites or their content.

No part of this publication may be reproduced, stored in a retrieval system, or transmitted in any form or by any means, electronic, mechanical, photocopying, recording, or otherwise, without written permission of the publisher. For information regarding permission, write to Nosy Crow Ltd., The Crow's Nest, 10a Lant St., London, SE1 1QR, United Kingdom.

This book is a work of fiction. Names, characters, places, and incidents are either the product of the author's imagination or are used fictitiously, and any resemblance to actual persons, living or dead, business establishments, events, or locales is entirely coincidental.

ISBN 978-0-545-84226-6

10 9 8 7 6 5 4   17 18 19 20

Printed in the U.S.A.   40
First printing 2016

Book design by Mary Claire Cruz

Zoe's Rescue Zoo

The Lucky Snow Leopard

Amelia Cobb

Illustrated by Sophy Williams

Scholastic Inc.

Chapter One
Christmas Comes to the Rescue Zoo

"Jingle Bells! Jingle Bells! Jingle all the way!" sang Zoe Parker, bursting through the door and dropping her schoolbag on the floor. "Meep, where are you? I'm home, and school's out for Christmas!"

Zoe's home was very unusual and very special. She lived in a little cottage, but it wasn't on a normal street. It was on the grounds of the Rescue Zoo—and Zoe's neighbors were the zoo animals!

There was a happy squeak from the kitchen and Zoe went to see what her best friend was up to. Meep was sitting on the kitchen table, nibbling a mini meat pie. He was a tiny gray mouse lemur with a long, curly tail and huge golden eyes. Today his playful little face was covered in crumbs! "Meep! I hope you haven't eaten all the mini pies again," said Zoe, trying not to laugh.

"Only two," chirped Meep happily.

2

"Christmastime is fun. There are so many tasty things to eat!"

Zoe scooped her friend up for a hug. "Come on, Meep. Mom and the zookeepers promised to wait until I was back from school before they decorate the Rescue Zoo Christmas tree!"

"Let's go!" squeaked Meep excitedly, bouncing out of Zoe's arms and scampering to the front door.

Together, the two friends raced through the zoo. The gates had closed early to visitors today so that the zoo staff could help with the decorations, and the path was empty and glittering with frost. The air was cold, and Christmas lights were strung along the fences, twinkling like stars. Zoe grinned as she walked along. Everything was starting to feel very

3

Christmassy—especially at the penguin
enclosure. This year, the keepers had
built a little ice skating rink next to the
penguins' home with a wooden hut
where visitors could borrow ice skates.

Zoe peered over the fence of the
enclosure and called out to the nearest
penguin. "Hi, Poppy! Do you know when
the ice skating rink opens?"

The little penguin waddled up to the
fence and squeaked back, flapping her
wings eagerly. "Ooh, tomorrow?" said
Zoe happily. "I can't wait to have a turn!"

Poppy tilted her head to one side and
squeaked curiously. "No, I've never done
it before," explained Zoe. "I don't think
I'll be very good, but it looks fun!"

Poppy waved a wing as Zoe and Meep
continued along the path. Zoe couldn't

help grinning as the lions roared to say hello, and the flamingos squawked a friendly greeting. This was the main reason Zoe loved her home at the zoo so much. She knew a very big secret: Animals understand every word people say and can talk to them. Most people don't understand their barks, squeals, and grunts—but Zoe did! She had never told anyone though. It was a special secret between her and her animal friends.

A few minutes later, Zoe and Meep stopped outside a brand-new enclosure. It wasn't open yet, and the gate was still boarded up with a big piece of wood. Zoe stood on her tiptoes to peek over the fence, and Meep climbed onto her head to get a better look. "Can you see anything, Meep?" asked Zoe hopefully.

"It's very big and I can see some trees and some rocks, but that's all," the little lemur chattered.

Zoe sighed. "I *wish* we knew what it was for!"

Not a single person at the Rescue Zoo knew what the new enclosure was for. A month ago, a postcard had arrived from Zoe's Great-Uncle Horace. In his messy handwriting, he'd asked the keepers at the zoo to build it and explained exactly what it should look like. But he hadn't said what animal would live there!

Great-Uncle Horace was the owner of
the Rescue Zoo. He was a famous
explorer, and he'd started the zoo because
of all the lost, injured, or frightened
animals he'd met on his adventures. Now
the Rescue Zoo was a safe home for
any creature in need. Zoe's mom was the
zoo vet, and they had lived in their little
cottage at the edge of the zoo since Zoe
was tiny. Great-Uncle Horace still traveled
around the world and brought new
animals back to the zoo whenever he
found them. Zoe hoped the mysterious
postcard meant he'd be home soon—along
with the zoo's newest member.

"I wonder what the new animal might
be, Meep," Zoe said, feeling a little bubble
of excitement in her tummy. "Imagine if
Great-Uncle Horace came home over the

holidays. That would make this the best Christmas ever!"

"He might arrive on Christmas Eve, just like Santa Claus!" chirped Meep enthusiastically.

"I just hope he comes back soon," Zoe added. "I really miss him."

Around the next corner was a park where visitors had picnics in the summer. But now, there was an enormous Christmas tree standing right in the middle of it. "Wow," breathed Zoe, staring up at the tree, which towered above her. "It's taller than our cottage, Meep. I think that's the biggest one we've ever had!"

Around it, the zookeepers were unpacking boxes of Christmas decorations. Zoe's mom was unwinding some tinsel. "There you are, Zoe!" she said, coming over to kiss her daughter's cheek. "Now we can get started!"

From the smiling faces around her, Zoe could tell that everyone was feeling very merry. The panda keeper, Stephanie, was walking around with a tray of mini pies, and the giraffe keeper, Frankie, was humming Christmas tunes. Zoe joined in with the song as she hung sparkly ornaments on the tree. "*Silent night, holy night, all is calm, all is bright!*"

"I want to help!" Meep chirped, tugging at the end of Zoe's scarf.

Zoe dropped her voice to a whisper so that no one would hear her talking to Meep. "Here," she said, placing a small, glittery ornament in his tiny paws. "Can you put this high up, where we can't reach?"

Meep nodded and scampered up the

tree. He hung the ornament on a branch and chattered proudly just as Zoe's mom glanced up. "Look! Smart Meep's helping us."

"It's almost as if he understands what to do," added Stephanie.

Zoe smiled to herself.

Finally, there was one decoration left. Zoe's heart sank as her mom unwrapped a shiny gold star. "Great-Uncle Horace *always* puts the star at the top of the tree," she said sadly. "We can't do it without him."

"Nonsense," snapped a voice behind her. Zoe groaned as Mr. Pinch, the horrible zoo manager, marched into the park. "*I'll* put up the star this year. I am in charge of the zoo while Mr. Higgins is away, after all," he announced importantly. Noticing all the boxes scattered around, he scowled. "Although if you ask me, Christmas makes far too much mess. All that nasty tinsel and wrapping paper everywhere?

 11

Ugh! I can't wait until it's over and everything's cleaned up again."

He tucked the gold star in his pocket and started climbing the ladder that the zookeepers had put next to the tree. Zoe frowned at him. Mr. Pinch was always complaining, but she couldn't believe he was even grumbling about Christmas!

Suddenly, a flash of blue appeared in the sky. It fluttered around the tree, landing gently on the highest branch. "Kiki!" cried Zoe, her heart thumping with excitement.

Kiki was a beautiful hyacinth macaw, with glossy feathers and a long, curved beak. She belonged to Great-Uncle Horace and went everywhere with him. "So that means . . ." began Zoe, looking around eagerly.

"Hello, everyone! I'm back!" called a cheerful voice.

Zoe and the crowd turned around, and everyone gasped. The Rescue Zoo reindeer, Ronny and Ruthie, were trotting into the park. They were pulling a huge sleigh behind them, which had the Rescue Zoo symbol, a colorful hot air balloon, painted on one side. Tucked inside the sleigh was a large wooden crate, and perched on the front seat was a beaming man with a white beard and a red wool hat.

"I see I'm just in time to put the star on the tree! You didn't think I'd miss it, did you?" he called cheerfully.

"Hooray!" cried Zoe, jumping up and down. "Great-Uncle Horace!"

Chapter Two
A Snowy Arrival

As Mr. Pinch started climbing back down the ladder, muttering angrily, the crowd rushed over to the sleigh. Zoe had never seen it before! She ran faster than anyone, and Great-Uncle Horace swept her into his arms for a big hug. "Zoe, my dear! I'm so happy to see you. It's wonderful to be home for Christmas!"

"This is one of the best presents I could have ever asked for!" replied Zoe, grinning. "But where have you been? Did you travel all the way on this sleigh?"

"Kiki and I have come from a very cold place called Mongolia," Great-Uncle Horace told her. "We got a plane home, but as we came through the zoo gates, we saw some of the zookeepers unpacking the new Rescue Zoo sleigh. I had it specially built so that visitors can have Christmas rides around the zoo! Isn't it great? Anyway, I guessed you'd be putting up the tree—so I thought I'd hop in the sleigh and surprise you all. Now—I think I'd better put up that star!"

He climbed out of the sleigh and Mr. Pinch grumpily handed over the star. Everyone watched as Great-Uncle

16

Horace carefully climbed the ladder and placed the star on top of the tree. "Lights, please!" he called down.

Zoe's mom switched the Christmas lights on, and the crowd cheered. The whole park was filled with a warm, cozy glow. Zoe had never seen the zoo look so pretty.

"It's beautiful!" she breathed.

When Great–Uncle Horace reached the
bottom of the ladder again, he clapped
his hands. "Now, I'm sure you've all
noticed that I've brought something home
with me," he announced, nodding to the
crate in the back of the sleigh. "And you
must have been wondering what the new
enclosure is for! Well, now I can show
you—if it's ready?"

Mr. Pinch looked annoyed. "I'd just like
to say, Mr. Higgins, that this enclosure
was *very* expensive to build. It was
extremely difficult to have it finished in
time, but we managed to—"

"So it *is* finished!" said Great–Uncle
Horace. "Excellent! Follow me, everyone."

He climbed back into the sleigh and
Zoe cuddled up happily next to him

18

with Meep on her shoulder. Her mind was buzzing as she wondered what the new animal could be. Meep was trying to guess too. "The crate's very big, Zoe, so the animal inside it must be too!" he chattered. "Maybe another giraffe? Or another polar bear!"

"It must be an animal we've never had at the Rescue Zoo before," Zoe pointed out in a whisper. "That's why the new enclosure had to be built!"

The reindeer trotted along gently, and Zoe could hear from their grunts that they were proud to be pulling the sleigh. In no time, they reached the new enclosure. The zookeepers arrived just behind them, and Great-Uncle Horace asked them to remove the wooden boards that kept it hidden.

As the enclosure was revealed slowly, Zoe gasped. It was enormous and very beautiful. Tall, craggy rocks stretched high into the air, with a sprinkling of snow at the top. There was a deep, cozy-looking cave tucked into the biggest rock, and a glittering waterfall that poured into a winding little stream.

"Brrr! It looks chilly in there, Zoe," squeaked Meep, shivering. "And those rocks look hard to walk on!"

"Maybe it's for some mountain goats? Perhaps the crate's so big because there are a lot of them?" Zoe whispered back. "I know they like the cold…"

Great-Uncle Horace asked for the
gates to be opened wide and the crate
carried inside the enclosure. Zoe thought
it looked very heavy. She held her breath
as two of the zookeepers unlocked the
crate and lowered one side of it to the
ground. There was a moment of silence as
everyone waited.

Then, a pair of huge, creamy-white
paws appeared, covered in black spots.
An elegant head peered out of the
crate and sniffed the air. Very slowly,
an enormous cat prowled out. A pattern
of dark spots covered her beautiful, fluffy
white coat.

"Zoe, what's that?" hissed Meep.

"A snow leopard!" Zoe said, gasping.

Great-Uncle Horace leaned toward
her, smiling widely. "Did you know

they are also known as 'ghosts of the
mountain' because they're so rare?" he
whispered.

Then there was a meow from inside the crate, and the pattering of smaller paws. Zoe couldn't believe her eyes as a second spotted face peeked out—but this time, it was a snow leopard *cub*!

Chapter Three
The Nervous Newcomers

The huge snow leopard stared at the crowd with icy blue eyes and swished her long, fluffy tail. She bared her sharp teeth and hissed fiercely. Everyone understood that this was a warning to stay away from her and her cub. The snow leopard cub huddled nervously between his mother's legs. Zoe could tell he wasn't a brand-new baby—he looked maybe three or four months old.

Zoe's mom took a cautious step toward the fence, but the snow leopard let out an angry growl and she stopped. "Oh, dear, they seem very anxious. I need to check them both over, but maybe I should leave them to settle in today."

Great-Uncle Horace nodded wisely. "The poor things have had quite a frightening time," he explained. "They were living on a lonely, snowy mountain when a farmer moved close by, along with his herd of sheep. The mother was hungry and desperate to feed her cub, so one night she took a sheep for them to eat for their dinner. When the farmer realized one was missing, he was very

angry. He would have killed them if Kiki
and I hadn't rescued them in time."

"Maybe that's why they don't seem to
like people very much?" Zoe said, gazing
at the snow leopards.

"I think you're right, my dear," sighed
Great-Uncle Horace.

The cub looked up at Zoe curiously,
but his mother prowled to the back of
the enclosure, settling down behind the
waterfall where she couldn't be seen. The
cub hesitated, and then followed quickly
after her.

I'll talk to them when no one's around,
Zoe thought. *Then they'll see that we're all
friendly here, and that no one wants to hurt
them.*

"Come on, Zoe. I think you've had
enough excitement for one day," her

mom said, smiling. "It's getting late, and there'll be plenty of time to get the snow leopards settled in over Christmas. Let's go home for a hot chocolate."

"I'll drop by later," Great-Uncle Horace promised.

Zoe couldn't stop thinking about the beautiful snow leopards as she and her mom walked back to the cottage. As they passed the elephant enclosure, she heard a little trumpet. Bertie, the baby elephant, was trying to get Zoe's attention.

"I'll catch up with you, Mom. I, um, left my mittens by the Christmas tree," Zoe said quickly, shoving her hands into her pockets. She didn't like not telling her mom the truth, but sometimes it was the only way she could talk to her animal friends.

28

"OK, Zoe. Don't be too long!" Zoe's mom said.

When her mom was out of sight, Zoe dashed over to the elephant enclosure, with Meep following closely behind her. She reached for the silver paw-print necklace she always wore and held it against the gate. With a click, the gate swung open. The necklace had been a special present from Great-Uncle Horace and opened every gate in the zoo!

Bertie rushed over to them, flapping his ears eagerly, and wrapped his little trunk around Zoe's waist. He was one of her favorite animals and always liked giving hugs! "You seem even more excited than usual, Bertie," Zoe laughed, stroking his head. "What are you so happy about today?"

Bertie let out a trumpet, and Zoe grinned. "It's almost Christmas, the zoo looks especially pretty, *and* you saw a big sleigh go past earlier?" she said. "You *have* had an exciting day, Bertie!"

Bertie squeaked curiously, and Zoe chuckled. "No, it wasn't Santa driving the sleigh. It was Great-Uncle Horace! He was coming home with two new animals for the zoo—a beautiful snow leopard and her cub. I suppose he did look a little like Santa, with his white beard and red hat! But there are still five nights left until Christmas, you know."

Bertie let out an impatient sigh, and Zoe smiled. "Listen, Bertie, Meep and I have to go home now. It's almost our bedtime! And if you go to sleep now too, it will soon be morning—and then there will only be *four* more nights until Christmas!"

Bertie's eyes grew wide, and he nodded eagerly. Zoe and Meep giggled as the little elephant dashed over to the trees he usually slept under, flung himself down on his cozy bed of hay and straw, and closed his eyes tightly. "I think Bertie wants it to be Christmas even more than we do, Meep!" Zoe whispered with a grin.

Chapter Four
Skating Fun!

"Mom, I'm already wearing a sweater!" laughed Zoe. "I don't need two!"

It was the next morning, and Zoe was getting ready for her first try at ice skating. Her mom had made her eat a big bowl of hot oatmeal and wrap up in a lot of layers. "Put this scarf on, then," she said, winding it around Zoe's neck. "You have to stay warm today. Ice skating is very chilly, and I don't want you to catch a cold for Christmas!"

Great-Uncle Horace arrived with a cheerful knock at the door. He was wearing a thick coat with a big, furry hood, and his nose was red from the cold. "You look snug, Zoe! This is my favorite coat for ice skating. It was a present from an Eskimo. It has a lot of useful pockets, so I've brought snacks in case we get hungry," he added, pulling out a cookie and crunching it happily.

"Will the ice skating rink be busy?" Zoe asked as they walked through the zoo. There were a lot of visitors today, dressed warmly and drinking cups of hot chocolate as they wandered around.

"Not today! I've decided that the rink

will just be for zoo staff today, as a special treat," explained Great-Uncle Horace. "Visitors can try it out tomorrow."

Zoe felt relieved. She was excited about ice skating, but she was glad it wouldn't be too crowded for her first try.

The rink was still empty when they arrived. Zoe stared at it shining in the morning sun. She thought that the perfectly smooth ice looked like a giant mirror. Great-Uncle Horace found a pair of ice skates in her size and showed her how to lace them up tightly. "You're ready! How would you like to be the first person on the ice?" he asked, helping her stand up.

"Yes please!" Zoe beamed. Then she looked down at her feet. "Oh . . . but I don't know how to do it!"

Great-Uncle Horace smiled. "Why don't you watch how the penguins slide along the ice?" he suggested, his eyes twinkling. "That might give you some ideas. I'll come and join you as soon as I've found some skates for myself!"

Zoe felt very wobbly. She held tight to the side of the rink and put one skate out onto the ice. "It's so slippery!" she told Meep, who was watching from the side.

"Maybe Goo is right!" squeaked Meep, using the funny nickname he had for Great-Uncle Horace. "Maybe you should see how the penguins do it."

"I could ask them for some tips!" said Zoe.

The penguins' home was on the other side of the fence. Zoe glanced around to check that Great-Uncle Horace was still busy searching for skates, then called out. "Polly! Pip! Everyone! Can you help me?"

The penguins waddled over, looking interested. "How do you stay up on the ice?" Zoe asked.

The littlest penguin, Pip, peeped proudly at Zoe. "OK, Pip, show me!" Zoe replied, smiling at the tiny penguin. She watched as he slid his small black feet out in front of him, one by one. Then she took a deep breath and slowly slid one skate forward a little bit, then another, with her arms out for balance.

"You're skating, Zoe!" Meep cried.

Zoe managed one very wobbly circle around the rink. "This is hard—but it's fun!" she said, grinning, as the penguins clapped their wings.

Then Great-Uncle Horace glided onto the ice. Zoe stared as he spun around in a circle. "I didn't know you were so good," she said.

"I learned to skate in Canada!" Great-Uncle Horace explained, taking Zoe's hand and skating along with her. Zoe suddenly felt much steadier with somebody to hold on to. "I was there to help a family of snowy owls—wonderful creatures. Did you know that male snowy owl feathers get whiter throughout their lives?"

As Zoe and Great-Uncle Horace skated around, the zookeepers started to join them. Even Mr. Pinch had come along. "This shouldn't be too difficult," he announced. But the moment he stepped onto the ice, his arms spun around in a

circle, his knees wobbled,
and his feet shot
out in opposite
directions.

"Oh,
dear,"
whispered
Great–
Uncle
Horace as
Mr. Pinch
fell flat on his bottom
with a noisy *thud*. Zoe heard the penguins
squeaking with laughter, and she tried to
hide her smile.

After a while Zoe's legs felt tired, so she
decided to take a break at the edge of
the rink. As she sat watching the others
skate, she had an idea. "Meep, why don't

we go and visit the snow leopards while everyone's busy here?" she whispered.

Zoe quickly swapped her skates for her boots, then she and Meep slipped away. The path outside the snow leopards' enclosure was closed to visitors for now because Great-Uncle Horace said they needed peace and quiet to get used to their new home. Zoe and Meep tiptoed past the NO ENTRY sign.

"Shall we use your necklace to go in, Zoe?" Meep asked.

Zoe hesitated. "Let's stay outside for now, Meep. The snow leopards don't know we want to be friends yet, and it might be dangerous."

They peered over the fence. It was very quiet, and all Zoe could hear was the trickle of the waterfall. "I can't see them!"

she whispered.

But Meep's sharp eyes had spotted something. "Look, Zoe! There's a long, fluffy tail peeking out from behind that bush."

"That must be the mom," said Zoe. "Great-Uncle Horace told me that snow leopards use their tails to keep their balance when they're climbing up mountains! I bet her cub is up there too. I wonder if they'll come and talk to us?" She took a deep breath and called, "Hello? My name's Zoe, and this is Meep."

The tail twitched, then disappeared. Then the mother snow leopard slowly peered out from behind the bush. After a second, her son's face appeared too. Zoe smiled hopefully, and the cub padded up to the fence. His mom watched suspiciously.

"Welcome to the Rescue Zoo," said Zoe. "We're so glad you've come to live here! What's your name?"

The cub meowed. "It's lovely to meet you, Ali," Zoe said. "And what's your mom called?"

Ali gave another meow, and Zoe smiled at the big snow leopard. "Hello, Lila," she called.

Before Zoe could say any more, the
mother snow leopard growled softly,
calling Ali away. The cub looked
disappointed, but leaped back across
the rocky ground and lay down next to
her. Zoe sighed. "Ali seems nice, but his
mom doesn't trust us yet, Meep," she said.
"At least we've said hello. That's a good
start—and we'll come back tomorrow to
try again!"

Chapter Five
The Sleepy Snow Leopard

"Come on, Meep!" said Zoe, rushing down the path. "I promised Great-Uncle Horace I'd help decorate the zoo staffroom this morning, but I want to go and see Ali again first."

The snow leopards had been at the Rescue Zoo for two days, and Zoe had gone to visit them every chance she got. She hadn't gone inside their enclosure yet though. Lila was still very protective of Ali.

When she arrived today, Ali was waiting for her. His eyes sparkled excitedly when he saw Zoe, and he gave a little growl, patting the fence with his paw. "Of course I want to come inside and play with you," exclaimed Zoe, feeling very excited. "But what about your mom? Did she say it was OK?"

Suddenly, Lila appeared from behind the waterfall and padded over to the fence. She growled solemnly, and Zoe nodded. "I promise we won't go too far," she replied. "Meep and I only want to make friends."

Lila nuzzled Ali with her big, furry

head, then disappeared back behind the
waterfall. Zoe grabbed her necklace
and opened the gate with Meep on her
shoulder. It felt strange to be inside the
beautiful enclosure when she'd only seen
it from the path!

Ali pounced straight on her boots and
she knelt down to play. She gave him a
big, furry cuddle, and then he wriggled
out of her arms and rolled onto his back

so that she could tickle his belly. His white fur was silky soft and covered in beautiful dark spots and splotches. Like his mom, he had bright blue eyes. Zoe thought he was one of the most beautiful animals she'd ever met.

Ali purred happily and licked Zoe's hand with his pink tongue. "It's lovely to finally play with you too!" giggled Zoe. "Do you like your enclosure? I bet you and your mom have been having a lot of fun splashing in the waterfall and playing hide-and-seek behind the rocks."

But Ali suddenly looked very sad and gave a miserable series of meows. Zoe frowned. "What do you mean, your mom won't play with you anymore?" she asked.

Ali glanced at his mom, who was curled up on a cozy ledge beside the waterfall.

She looked fast asleep. His tail drooping sadly, Ali explained that they used to play a lot—but now his mom just wanted to sleep all the time.

Zoe stroked his furry little head. "Poor Ali," said Zoe. "I think she's just tired from the journey. But I'll ask my mom to come and give her a checkup just in case. She's a doctor especially for animals, and she'll know if anything's wrong."

Ali purred as she tickled his ears, and Zoe decided she'd speak to her mom that morning. Her mom still hadn't examined the snow leopards because she'd been giving them time to settle in. But if Lila was sick, it was important to find out right away.

"It's so good that you got here in time for Christmas!" Zoe told the little cub.

Ali tilted his head and meowed curiously, a puzzled look on his face. Zoe and Meep gasped. "Really? You've never heard of Christmas?" squeaked Meep.

Ali tilted his head, and Meep nearly fell over in surprise. Zoe giggled. "Well, you just wait," she told the cub. "You're going to love it!"

Chapter Six
Some Exciting News

"What do you think, Great-Uncle Horace?" asked Zoe, holding up a paper snowflake. "We learned how to make these at school. You just fold up some white paper, cut out tiny pieces carefully with scissors, then open them up flat again and you've made a pattern! I think this is my best one so far!"

"You're doing an excellent job there, my dear," replied Great-Uncle Horace, who was putting up some sparkly lights around the door. "The staffroom is going to look wonderful once we've finished decorating. Shall I help you tape the snowflakes to the window?"

"I think I can reach!" said Zoe. "And smart Meep has already got the tape ready," she added, winking at her little friend.

"Oh no. More mess!" snapped Mr. Pinch as he walked in. "If it's going to be all Christmassy in here too, I think I'll go and sit by myself in my office. You won't find any decorations *there*."

"Come along now, Percy! You have to admit, the zoo looks splendid," said Great-Uncle Horace.

 51

Mr. Pinch frowned. "I have never understood why people get so excited about Christmas," he said frostily. "All the fuss about presents! The horrible pies! The awful songs!"

"You must like Christmas carols though," said Great-Uncle Horace, sounding shocked. "Everyone likes carols, Percy! What about the wonderful carol concert here at the Rescue Zoo on Christmas Eve?"

"Christmas songs make my ears hurt," grumbled Mr. Pinch in reply. "And mistletoe makes me sneeze. Now, if you'll excuse me."

He stomped off toward his office. Great-Uncle Horace sighed, and then his face lit up. "I have an idea! I'm going to sneak after him and hang this wreath on his

office door," he whispered, winking at
Zoe. "We'll just have to change his mind
about Christmas. Back in a minute!"

As soon as he left, Zoe shook her head.
"Meep, can you believe how grumpy
Mr. Pinch is?"

"He doesn't even like *presents*!" chattered
Meep in disbelief. "But opening presents
is so exciting. I love ripping open the
wrapping paper and seeing what's inside!"

"What do you hope Santa brings you
this year, Meep?" Zoe asked, scooping
her little friend up for a hug. "I wrote
and asked for a bracelet with a lot of
pretty animal charms on it. I even drew a
picture of it in my letter!"

"I'd like three bananas, two apples, a
bag of peanuts, some nice, juicy raisins,
a tub of yummy strawberries, a lot of

sunflower seeds…" said Meep.

Zoe laughed. "Meep, everything you've asked for is food!"

"I like food," Meep told her very seriously.

The door burst open and Great-Uncle Horace strode back in—followed by Zoe's mom. "I bumped into your mom on the way back from Mr. Pinch's office," said Great-Uncle Horace. "She says she has some exciting news for us!"

Zoe's mom was beaming. "I wanted to tell you both together. Zoe, after you called me at the zoo hospital this morning, I went to give the snow leopards a checkup. By the way, I love the names you picked for them! And I'm pleased to say that Lila and Ali are perfectly healthy."

"That's excellent news!" said Great-

Uncle Horace.

"And there's more!" she continued. "Lila has been sleeping all the time for a reason. She's pregnant! And she should be giving birth very soon!"

Zoe gasped. "I can't believe it. Ali's going to have some little brothers or sisters!" So that was why Lila was so tired all the time!

"And the Rescue Zoo will have a whole

family of snow leopards!" cried Great-
Uncle Horace, throwing his hat into
the air. "What a wonderful Christmas
surprise!"

While Zoe rushed to the snow leopard
enclosure with her mom and Great-
Uncle Horace, Meep raced around the
zoo spreading the news. Soon the air was
filled with excited barks, tweets, roars, and
grunts of celebration.

Lila was nowhere to be seen, until Zoe
caught a glimpse of spotted white fur in
the cave. "Look, she's up there!" she said.

"Well spotted, Zoe! It looks like she's
chosen the cave as her den," said Great-
Uncle Horace, nodding thoughtfully. "A
lot of shelter, and it's warm and dry. That's
where Lila will bring up her new babies
for the first few months of their lives."

"I can't wait," said Zoe, grinning. "The new cubs will be so tiny and furry and cute! I love it when babies are born at the zoo."

"All we can do now is wait," her mom said, smiling at Zoe. "How exciting! It's strange, but the animals seem to understand that something's happening," she added. "Have you noticed they're all really noisy today?"

"Yes, very odd," said Great-Uncle Horace, and Zoe thought there was a funny twinkle in his eyes. "Now, I think I'd like a mini pie to celebrate the news! Would you like one, Zoe?"

Zoe was about to say yes, but caught sight of a spotted tail poking out from behind a tree. Ali! "I'll be there in a minute," she said quickly.

As Great-Uncle Horace and Zoe's mom walked off, Zoe used her necklace to slip inside the enclosure and dashed over to Ali. "I've just heard!" she cried. "You're going to be a big brother! Aren't you excited?"

To her surprise, Ali gave a sad little meow and buried his face in his paws. Zoe couldn't believe it. "What do you mean, you don't want to be a big brother?" she asked. "Why not?"

Sniffling, Ali glanced sadly up at the cave

where his mom was resting. Zoe reached out to give him a hug. "Don't worry, Ali. Your mom will be able to play with you again soon, and she's never going to forget about you, even when the new babies come along! She'll love you just as much."

Ali shook his little head, and Zoe tried again. "Just think about how fun it's going to be! You're really lucky, Ali."

But it was no use. Ali meowed a glum good-bye and padded behind the waterfall to lie down by himself. Zoe stared after him, her heart sinking. It seemed like everyone was excited about the new cubs—except for their big brother!

Chapter Seven
The Sad Little Snow Leopard

As Zoe lay in bed that night with Meep cuddled by her feet, she couldn't stop thinking about Ali. How could she make the sad little cub see that having brothers and sisters would be fun, and that his mom wouldn't forget about him?

At breakfast time, she was very quiet as

she nibbled her toast. "Is anything wrong, Zoe?" her mom asked.

Zoe shook her head. She couldn't explain why she was worried, because her mom didn't know she could talk to animals! "I'm going to have another peek at the snow leopards this morning," she said.

"Good idea, Zoe. Come and tell me right away if you think the babies might be coming!" her mom said.

Zoe walked to the snow leopards' enclosure with Meep on her shoulder, thinking about what to say to Ali. On the way, she passed the path that led to Higgins Hall, the huge manor house where Great-Uncle Horace lived. It was set on a hill overlooking the zoo. Most of the big, old rooms had been turned into

animal enclosures when Great-Uncle
Horace opened the zoo, so the kitchen
was jumping with frogs, and thousands of
butterflies fluttered around the ballroom!
Great-Uncle Horace had just kept the
attic for Kiki and himself.

Zoe looked up at the Hall and noticed
that a crowd had gathered on the lawn
outside. "Meep, let's go and find out
what's going on up there!" she said.

As they reached the Hall, Zoe spotted
a lot of cameras and microphones.
"They're reporters, Meep—and it sounds
like they've come to ask Great-Uncle
Horace about Lila giving birth," she
whispered.

Great-Uncle Horace was standing in
front of the crowd, answering questions.
Zoe smiled as she noticed that he was

wearing tinsel around his neck like a scarf. "Oh yes, we're very excited," Great-Uncle Horace was saying. "Snow leopards are incredibly rare. Did you know that there are only a few thousand left in the world?"

"Mr. Higgins, do you think they might arrive on Christmas Day?" one reporter called out.

Great-Uncle Horace beamed. "Wouldn't that be splendid? We'll just have to wait and see!"

Zoe and Meep slipped away quietly and walked toward the snow leopards' enclosure. The path outside it was now open to visitors, but there was a big sign saying OUR NEW BABY SNOW LEOPARDS ARE COMING SOON. PLEASE TRY TO BE QUIET SO THEIR MOTHER CAN REST!

A family was talking in hushed voices. "I can see the mother asleep in that cave," whispered a man with red glasses. "But where's the cub?"

Suddenly, in a blur of black-and-white fur, Ali appeared from a little space in the rocks. He dashed up the cliff toward the cave and pounced on his sleeping mom with a playful meow. Lila's eyes flew open and she growled in surprise. Ali patted her head with his paws, purring hopefully.

"He wants to play!" Zoe whispered to Meep.

But Lila grunted and rolled over, closing her eyes again. The cub kept jumping on her until Lila snarled at him angrily.

"Oh, dear, looks like he's in trouble with his mom!" chuckled the man.

Sulkily, Ali padded out of the cave, his tail low. He sat by himself next to the stream, a little scowl on his face. The family wandered off, chatting about which animal to see next, and Zoe and Meep slipped inside the enclosure and rushed over to Ali.

"You know your mom needs to rest before the babies arrive," said Zoe, crouching down next to him. "That was naughty of you."

Ali growled angrily. "I know you don't want any brothers or sisters," Zoe replied softly, "but I bet you'd change your mind if you met some of the other families at the Rescue Zoo. Chi Chi and Mei Mei are pandas, and they're twin sisters. They're always having fun together. They love playing tricks—especially on Mr. Pinch! Then there's Otto and Benedict, the baby otters. They're brothers *and* best friends!"

Ali meowed curiously. "No, I don't have any brothers or sisters," Zoe explained. "I wish I did! I'm really lucky, though, because I have Meep to be my best friend!"

"And we have all our other animal friends too!" added Meep.

"Cheer up, Ali," Zoe said, smiling at the cub. "You can't be sad when Christmas is just two nights away!"

Ever since Ali had found out about Christmas, he'd wanted to know all about it. Zoe and Meep had explained about the Christmas carol concert, the ice skating rink, and all the pretty decorations, and Ali had listened in amazement. When Zoe had told him about the beautiful Christmas tree, he'd leaped to the highest rocky peak in his enclosure to see if he could spot it, and purred with delight when he saw the glittering gold star.

"Tomorrow is Christmas Eve," Zoe went on. "That's when Santa Claus comes."

Ali meowed excitedly. "No, he's not a snow leopard!" giggled Zoe. "He's a human, like me."

Ali held up a front paw and meowed again. "Oh, no! He doesn't *have* claws," laughed Zoe. "That's just his name."

"He brings presents!" chirped Meep, hopping up and down.

Ali gave a hopeful little squeak. "Yes, he might bring you a present too!" said Zoe. "But only if you're good and let your mom sleep."

Ali glanced up at Lila sleeping in the cave and gave a grumpy growl.

Quickly, Zoe tried to change the subject back to something more fun. "What do you want for Christmas, Ali?" she asked

70

cheerfully. "Some toys or something yummy to eat?"

But Zoe's heart sank as Ali gave a sulky snarl in reply. Ali didn't want presents for Christmas—he just wanted to keep his mom all to himself!

Chapter Eight
Christmas Carols

"There, all done! Now it's time for the
carol concert," said Zoe, hanging up
the last stocking outside the giraffe
enclosure. She and the zookeepers had
walked around the whole zoo that
afternoon, putting up a stocking for every
animal. Bertie the little elephant had
trumpeted with excitement when he saw

his stocking, which had a big blue "B" sewn onto it. "Of course I'll come and see what's inside it tomorrow!" Zoe had promised him.

It was a cold evening and the sky twinkled with stars. The zoo was open late on Christmas Eve so that visitors could stay for the concert, and there was an excited feeling in the air. Some of the zookeepers were handing out cups of hot chocolate and gingerbread, and everyone was smiling.

The concert was always held in front of the huge Christmas tree. When Zoe arrived, her mom was pacing up and down anxiously. "I'm a little nervous," she explained to Zoe. "Great-Uncle Horace has asked me to start off the singing this year, so I'm doing the first verse by myself."

Zoe helped her mom hand out sheets of paper with the words to the songs on them so that everyone could sing along. There was a big crowd now, with Great-Uncle Horace and Kiki right at the front. When the crowd fell silent, her mom coughed nervously and started to sing, in a rather shaky voice, "*We wish you a merry Christmas, we wish you a merry Christmas . . .*"

"*We wish you a merry Christmas, and a happy new year!*" Zoe sang, grinning at her mom. The rest of the crowd joined in right away, and soon everyone was singing at the tops of their voices.

Everyone except Mr. Pinch! Zoe noticed him standing moodily at the back, wearing earplugs to block out the music. *Grumpy old thing*, thought Zoe.

When the last song was finished, everyone clapped and cheered. As the crowd began to trickle toward the exit, chattering happily, Great-Uncle Horace called, "Merry Christmas, everyone! Thank you for coming!"

"That was fun," said Zoe's mom, beaming. "We'd better get back to the cottage, I think. It's time to hang your stocking up, Zoe!"

"Are you going to sleep at the cottage tonight too?" Zoe asked Great-Uncle Horace hopefully. Last year, Great-Uncle Horace had stayed over on Christmas Eve because he'd given his attic room at the Hall to a meerkat with an earache so that the poor animal could sleep somewhere peaceful and quiet until he got better.

"Of course! It's a Christmas tradition

now. And that way, I get to spend the
whole day with my two favorite people,"
replied Great-Uncle Horace. "Besides,
I'm not sure Santa would get down the
chimney at Higgins Hall. The last time I
checked, some naughty puffins had built
their nest inside it!"

As Mr. Pinch marched past, Zoe's mom
called out to him. "Mr. Pinch, wait a
second! I want to ask you something."
She took a deep breath. "I just wondered
if you'd like to have Christmas dinner
with us tomorrow?"

Zoe looked at her mom in horror, and
Meep gave a squeak of disbelief. Even
Great-Uncle Horace seemed surprised.
Mr. Pinch stared at Zoe's mom. "Me?"
he said. "Why?"

"Because it's Christmas!" she said. "I

know you don't like it very much, but you can't spend the whole day by yourself. Please come; we'd like to spend it with you."

Mr. Pinch hesitated. "Well . . . I, uh, suppose I could stop by for a little while."

Blushing, Mr. Pinch rushed off to his office. Zoe and Great-Uncle Horace turned to her mom, who sighed. "Look, I know Mr. Pinch can be difficult, but no one should be alone at Christmas."

Meep was in a serious sulk. "Christmas is going to be ruined," the little lemur grumbled.

"At least we'll have fun in the morning, before he arrives," whispered Zoe, trying her best to stay cheerful. Deep down, she felt really disappointed. Mr. Pinch had made it very clear that he didn't

. 0. 02

. 0. 0....

like Christmas. She just knew he would complain all day long. It wasn't going to be the same with him there.

On the way home, Zoe remembered something. She had one last job to do! "I'll see you at home," she told her mom, and ran over to the ice skating rink with Meep scampering beside her. That afternoon, she'd hidden something in the wooden shed where the skates were kept—a present for Ali. "Let's give it to him now, Meep," she said, tucking the present under her arm. "I know it's not Christmas until tomorrow, but it might cheer him up."

When they arrived at his enclosure, the little cub was curled up on a rock. "Look, Ali," Zoe called as she used her necklace to open the gate. "We've brought you a present!" She showed him the present and then helped him pull off the wrapping paper. Underneath was a colorful ball. "It's covered in spots, like you!" she said.

Ali stared at the ball. He gave it a little push with his paw and meowed excitedly as it rolled along. Zoe grinned—Ali loved it!

Zoe and Meep took turns bouncing the ball to Ali and laughed as he chased happily after it. Then Meep made Zoe and Ali giggle by jumping on the ball

and showing them how many somersaults
he could turn without falling off! Before
long, Zoe realized it was getting late.
"We'd better go home, Meep. Mom will
be wondering where we are," she said.

To her
surprise, Ali
let out a
miserable
meow.
"What's
wrong?"
cried Zoe.
"You were
so happy a
minute ago!"

Ali looked sadly at the ball
and whimpered. "I'm sorry, Ali. I wish we
could stay and play too," Zoe told him.

"You know we can't be here *all* the time, even though we'd like to."

The cub gave another small meow. "Of course you won't have to play with the ball all by yourself!" Zoe said. "Meep and I will come back tomorrow, I promise."

But that didn't help to cheer up poor Ali. He padded away behind a tree, sniffling, and Zoe and Meep couldn't coax him out. Eventually they gave up and decided to go home, feeling a little worried. How could she get Ali to realize how lucky he was?

"Oh, dear, Zoe. You look very sad!" said Great-Uncle Horace as she and Meep came into the cottage.

"I hope you're not too upset with me for inviting Mr. Pinch tomorrow," Zoe's mom said. "I promise we'll still have a good day." She gave Zoe a big hug. "I know what will cheer you up. Why don't we hang up our stockings?"

Zoe's mom quickly went up into the attic to get the special box they kept the stockings in. "Here's yours, Zoe!" her mom said, pulling it out and handing it to her. "And Great-Uncle Horace, here are yours and Kiki's. Mine's next . . . and let's not forget Meep's, of course," she said with a grin.

Zoe hung her stocking over the fireplace, with Meep's next to it. Zoe's mom pinned hers next to Meep's, and Great-Uncle Horace added his and Kiki's. They looked very nice, all hanging in a colorful line! Then Zoe put a meat pie and a carrot on a plate and placed it carefully in front of the fireplace.

 83

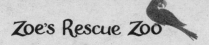

"Santa will be on his way now, Zoe," her mom said, smiling. "I wonder what he'll bring?"

Zoe sighed. She just hoped Ali would cheer up in time for Christmas Day.

"Hopefully he'll bring the zoo a little Christmas cheer," she said, and her mom smiled.

"I thought you were desperate for *another* present from Santa?" her mom replied, winking at Zoe.

Zoe remembered the charm bracelet she was longing for and grinned. "Well, I'd really like that too!" she said.

Chapter Nine
Mr. Pinch's Present

"Zoe, wake up! It's Christmas!"

Zoe's eyes flew open. Meep was bouncing on her pillow, chattering excitedly. "It's Christmas! It's Christmas!"

Zoe leaped out of bed and dashed down the stairs, shouting for her mom and Great-Uncle Horace. Santa Claus had been here! The mini pie was nothing but crumbs, the carrot was completely gone, and the stockings on the mantelpiece were fat with presents. There were even some brightly wrapped presents under the tree. Zoe and Meep danced with excitement as her mom and Great-Uncle Horace came in, yawning but looking pleased. Kiki was perched on Great-Uncle Horace's shoulder, squawking happily.

"Merry Christmas!" said Great-Uncle Horace, beaming. "Goodness, that stocking of mine looks very exciting. I wonder if Santa has brought the cookies I asked for?"

Everyone took turns opening a present. First Zoe unwrapped a colorful book about dolphins. Then there was a box of chocolates shaped like penguins and a pair of pink pajamas with a pattern of tiny snow leopards. "They look just like Ali!" said Zoe, beaming.

Zoe loved her presents, but she couldn't help feeling a bit disappointed. Santa hadn't brought her the bracelet she'd wanted after all. She tried hard not to mind and opened her chocolates to offer them around. Then her mom said, "Hold on, Zoe—I think you've missed one." She pointed at the toe of Zoe's stocking. There was something small and square stuffed inside it.

Zoe reached inside her stocking and pulled out a little red box tied with a gold ribbon. As she opened it, something gleamed and twinkled in the light from the Christmas tree. "My bracelet!" she cried, taking it carefully out of the box. It was silver, with tiny lion, elephant, and giraffe charms. "Santa brought me my bracelet!"

"I knew he would!" her mom said with a smile. "You've been so good this year, Zoe."

Zoe's mom unwrapped a new bag to keep all her animal medicines in. "Just what I wanted!" she said. And Zoe proudly gave Great-Uncle Horace a special present wrapped in zebra-patterned paper. "This is from me and Mom," she said.

"Although it was Zoe's idea," her mom added.

Great-Uncle Horace pulled off the
wrapping paper. "A compass!" he
exclaimed, holding it up. "And look, the
Rescue Zoo hot air balloon is engraved
on the back!"

"It's so you'll always find your way
home from your travels," Zoe explained.

"It's the best present I've ever gotten,"
Great-Uncle Horace said sincerely.

Zoe felt like she might burst with
happiness.

"Where's Meep?" asked Zoe's mom,
looking around.

There was a funny munching sound
coming from Meep's stocking. Zoe peeked
inside and giggled. The little lemur had
climbed right in and was tucking into his
Christmas presents! "Meep, don't eat them
all at once," Zoe whispered when her

 90

mom and Great-Uncle Horace were busy chatting. "You'll get a tummy ache."

Meep didn't seem to mind. "Yum!" he replied, nibbling happily on another nut.

Kiki was enjoying her stocking too. The clever macaw perched on the mantelpiece with her strong claws, bent right down, and tugged her presents out with her beak. Santa had brought her a bag of nuts, three juicy carrots, and some wooden toys that she could chew on to keep her beak healthy.

Once Zoe had helped clean up the wrapping paper, she got dressed and headed out into the zoo. All the zookeepers were there already, wearing cheerful Christmas sweaters. There was still a lot of work to do, just like any other day! Zoe rushed around helping—she

91

carried bags of nuts to the monkeys
and boxes of mangoes to the fruit bats.
Everyone was having an especially tasty
breakfast on Christmas morning.

Great-Uncle Horace put on some
Christmas music and everyone sang
loudly. Zoe was astonished to hear

Mr. Pinch humming along too when he thought no one was paying attention. "Are you enjoying the music, Mr. Pinch?" she asked.

Mr. Pinch blushed. "Err—no! I just had a tickle in my throat," he said quickly, marching off.

Zoe tried to wish all her animal friends a merry Christmas, but there wasn't enough time to visit everyone. Before long, her mom was calling, "Zoe! It's time to start making Christmas dinner."

"But we haven't been to see Ali yet!" chirped Meep.

"We'll go after we've eaten," whispered Zoe.

Back at the cottage, Zoe's mom had put a big turkey in the oven, and Great-Uncle Horace and Zoe peeled potatoes. The radio was playing more Christmas music, and it was warm and cozy in the kitchen. Suddenly there was a knock at the door. "That will be Mr. Pinch," her mom said. "Will you go and let him in, Zoe?"

Zoe took a deep breath as she opened the door. *Please let Mr. Pinch be nice today,* she thought hopefully.

Mr. Pinch was standing on the doorstep, wearing a green sweater with a Christmas tree on it. He was clutching a pile of presents. Zoe was surprised to see that he looked nervous. "Hello," she said.

"Hello," Mr. Pinch said, a little stiffly.

"Merry Christmas!" said Zoe's mom as Zoe and Mr. Pinch walked into the kitchen.

"We're very glad to see you, Percy," Great-Uncle Horace added warmly.

Meep blew a very rude raspberry noise. "Shhh, Meep!" hissed Zoe, hoping Mr. Pinch hadn't heard.

"Thank you for asking me," Mr. Pinch said awkwardly. "Um, what shall I do?"

Zoe's mom handed him a peeler and a bag of carrots. "If you could peel those, that would be nice. If we all join in, dinner will be ready in no time!"

Mr. Pinch nodded and got to work. It was quiet for the next few minutes, until Zoe's favorite carol came on the radio. "I love this one!" said Zoe, singing along. "*Rudolph the red-nosed reindeer had a very shiny nose . . .*"

"*And if you ever saw him, you would even say it glows!*" burst out Mr. Pinch.

Everyone turned to stare at him. "I thought you didn't like carols, Mr. Pinch!" said Zoe's mom.

Mr. Pinch blushed. "Well, I don't mind *that* one too much," he murmured.

When the vegetables had been peeled and chopped, Zoe's mom went to check on the turkey while Great–Uncle Horace put the finishing touches to the enormous trifle he had made for dessert. Mr. Pinch and Zoe set the table together, with a red napkin and a sparkly party popper next to everyone's plate. There was even a seat for Meep.

Zoe tried to think of something to say to Mr. Pinch. She caught sight of the bracelet on her wrist. "Look, Mr. Pinch—this is what Santa brought me," she said, holding her hand up to show him. "All the charms are different animals that we have in the zoo."

"Very nice," Mr. Pinch said awkwardly. "Actually, I brought you a small gift too, Zoe."

He handed Zoe a present wrapped neatly in silver paper. "Oh! Thank you," Zoe said uncertainly, glancing at Meep. *A present from Mr. Pinch?* she thought. *What could it be?*

She pulled off the paper—and gasped.

Inside was a Rescue Zoo uniform just
like the ones the zookeepers wore, but in
just the right size for Zoe! "Uh, I had it
specially made," Mr. Pinch explained, his
cheeks pink. "It's for when you're helping
out around the zoo, so that the visitors
know you're officially allowed to be there.

We, um, we wouldn't want people getting the wrong idea. They might think we let just any children help out."

Zoe couldn't believe it. "I love it!" she said, giving Mr. Pinch a big hug. The zoo manager looked surprised and a little bit embarrassed, but Zoe thought he seemed quite pleased too. Even though Mr. Pinch was still a little grumpy, his present really meant a lot to her. "I'm going to wear it right now," she said.

Zoe ran up to her bedroom to put the uniform on. She caught sight of herself in the mirror and couldn't help grinning. She really *did* look like a real zookeeper! When she came back downstairs, Zoe's mom made her and Mr. Pinch stand next to the Christmas tree together and took a picture. "Lovely! That's such a thoughtful gift, Mr. Pinch," she said, smiling. "Now, everyone sit down—dinner's ready."

"It smells delicious!" said Mr. Pinch, sounding really happy. Zoe and Meep glanced at each other and grinned. They'd never seen Mr. Pinch in such a good mood before. "It looks like Mr. Pinch does like Christmas after all," Meep whispered in Zoe's ear.

Great-Uncle Horace

put slices of steaming turkey on
everyone's plate, and Zoe's mom dished out
roast potatoes, vegetables, and gravy. As
they ate, Great-Uncle Horace
told exciting stories
from his travels.
Zoe and Mr.
Pinch helped
themselves
to seconds,
and they
all pulled
their
party
poppers
noisily.
Everyone
put on the
paper crowns

that fell out and took turns reading the jokes out loud.

"What do you get if you cross Santa with a duck?" asked Zoe's mom, grinning.

"I know this one. A Christmas quacker!" chuckled Great-Uncle Horace.

"This is a good one!" said Mr. Pinch. "What animal drops from the clouds?"

Everyone thought carefully. "Hmm, that's hard," said Zoe. "An animal that drops from the clouds . . ."

"I know! I know!" Meep bounced up and down on his chair, squeaking. "It's a reindeer, Zoe! Get it? *Rain* deer!"

Zoe giggled. The clever little lemur was right! "Is it a reindeer?" she asked.

But Mr. Pinch was gazing out the window. "Snow!" he said.

"What?" said Zoe, puzzled. "That doesn't make sense."

"No, look!" replied Mr. Pinch, pointing outside. "Snow! It's snowing!"

Chapter Ten
White Christmas

"I can't believe it. It's a white Christmas!"
cried Zoe's mom as everyone rushed to
the window. Mr. Pinch was right—snow
was swirling down softly, and there was
already a glittery white layer covering
the path.

"It's so pretty!" said Zoe.

"I wonder what the animals will think?"

said Mr. Pinch.

Suddenly, Zoe thought of Lila and Ali. They had come from one of the snowiest places in the world. Maybe the snow would remind them of their home! "Mom, can I go out for a little while?" she asked.

Her mom smiled. "Of course! We probably need a break before dessert anyway. Make sure you wrap up though, and don't be too long."

Zoe flung her coat on over her new uniform and ran outside. She jumped around happily outside the cottage, kicking up little clouds of powdery snow with her boots. "I *love* walking in the snow, Meep," she exclaimed. "It's so pretty. And it makes such a nice, crunchy sound!"

"But it's so cold, Zoe!" squeaked a little voice behind her. Meep was perched on the front step of the cottage, looking very uncertainly at the snow. He dipped a little paw in it and shivered. "It *looks* like a nice, soft blanket . . . but it feels all wet!"

"I'll carry you, Meep," said Zoe, scooping her friend up so that he could sit on her shoulders.

A lot of the animals were unsure about the snow too. The marmoset monkeys were huddled together under a big tree, and the giant tortoise, Charles, had pulled his wrinkly old head back into his shell so that it wouldn't get cold. But some of them loved it! Bella the baby polar bear was rolling around in it, squealing gleefully. The playful chimpanzees were throwing snowballs at each other, and the hippos were sticking out their tongues and catching snowflakes. "It's a little like

eating ice cream straight from the sky!"
Zoe giggled.

When Zoe and Meep reached the snow leopards' enclosure and went inside, they couldn't see Lila or Ali—but there was a deep purring sound coming from the cave and a high, happy squeak. "It sounds like they're pleased about the snow, Meep!" said Zoe.

Just then, Ali's little face popped out of the cave, and he meowed excitedly. "OK, we'll climb up!" replied Zoe, grinning at the eager cub. "What have you got to show us?"

The cub just purred playfully and disappeared again. Zoe and Meep glanced at each other, puzzled, and climbed the rocky path up to the cave.

Lila was curled up inside, with Ali sitting proudly next to her. And cuddled up between them, yawning sleepily, were *three* tiny, beautiful snow leopard babies! They had little flat ears and sweet pink paws.

Zoe gasped. "*This* is what you wanted
to show us. I can't believe it, Ali. The
babies have been born—on Christmas
Day! And there are three of them! They're
so beautiful. Are they boys or girls?"

Lila gave a deep, contented growl. "Wow," breathed Zoe. "You've got three little sisters, Ali! Aren't you lucky!"

Ali swished his fluffy tail happily. Zoe felt a little tug on her sleeve and turned to see Meep looking puzzled. "What is it, Meep?" she whispered.

"Why is Ali so happy about the babies?" chattered Meep. "He definitely didn't want to be a big brother before!"

Ali gave another happy meow. "The *ball* changed your mind?" repeated Zoe. "You mean the one we gave you as a present? But why?"

"You were sad about the ball yesterday, Ali, because we couldn't stay and play," added Meep.

Ali looked at his little sisters and purred softly. Zoe grinned. "Now it all makes sense," she said. "Because now that the babies are here, it means you'll always have someone to play with!"

Meep squeaked happily and Zoe smiled. She was glad to see Ali had changed his mind!

Chapter Eleven
Snowy Sisters

Zoe watched as Lila cleaned the babies' little heads carefully with her tongue. Ali purred loudly as she leaned over and gave him a big lick too.

"See, Ali," said Zoe, smiling. "You're still just as important to your mom, even now that the babies are here."

"What are they going to be named?"

chirped Meep.

Lila looked at Ali and gave a gentle growl. Ali's eyes opened very wide, and Zoe grinned. "Ali—you're allowed to choose their names! You're so lucky. What are you going to call them?"

Ali looked at his sisters, wrinkling his nose as he thought. Then his ears pricked and he meowed excitedly. "Those are great names, Ali!" Zoe exclaimed. "And they're perfect for babies born on Christmas Day. Listen, Meep and I have to go and tell everyone the news. We'll be back as soon as we can!"

Zoe raced back to the cottage, shouting to all her animal friends as she passed them. "The snow leopard babies are here! Three girl cubs!"

"Tell everyone!" added Meep, dashing

along next to her.

They burst into the cottage and made everyone jump. "Zoe, there you are! We're just about to have dessert," said her mom, scooping trifle into bowls. "Come and sit down."

"I can't! The snow leopard cubs have been born," Zoe gasped, breathless from running so fast.

Zoe's mom dropped her spoon, and Great-Uncle Horace and Mr. Pinch leaped up from the table. "I don't believe it!" she said, grabbing her coat and her special new vet bag. "Quick—we'd better run over there to check that they're OK."

They hurried back along the path, following the footprints Zoe and Meep had already made in the snow. Kiki flew ahead of them, squawking eagerly. By now the zoo was alive with excited roars, hoots, grunts, and whinnies, and a lot of the animals were chatting to their neighbors about the new arrivals. Zoe couldn't wait to talk to them all about the cubs later.

When they got back to the enclosure, Kiki was perched on the fence and Ali was waiting for them at the gate. Everyone climbed up to the cave and peeked inside. The babies had fallen asleep, cuddled up together in a fluffy heap, their little bellies marked with tiny dark spots, rising and falling. Lila was watching them proudly. "Oh, they're beautiful," whispered Zoe's mom. "I wonder what we should call them."

"I've already thought of some names," Zoe said quickly. "Snowy, Holly, and Ivy!"

"Excellent—Christmas names!" exclaimed Great-Uncle Horace.

"I wonder if Lila will let me check them," Zoe's mom said hopefully.

"I think she will," said Zoe, glancing at Lila, and the big leopard gave a friendly purr. Very carefully, Zoe's mom picked the first sleeping cub up. "It's a girl!" She smiled. "She looks perfect. She's so soft!"

"Snow leopard cubs are always born with a full coat of their beautiful fur," Great-Uncle Horace told Zoe. "They won't open their eyes for the first week of their lives, just like a kitten. But when they do, I bet they'll be a beautiful bright blue just like their mother's."

"And their big brother's!" added Zoe, smiling over at Ali, who gave a happy meow.

Zoe noticed Mr. Pinch wiping his eyes and pulling a handkerchief out of his sleeve. "Are you all right, Mr. Pinch?" she asked.

Mr. Pinch sneezed twice and blew his nose noisily. "I'm allergic to cats," he explained. It sounded like he had a bad cold.

Zoe held her breath and waited for

Mr. Pinch to grumble and complain angrily. But instead, he reached out to give one of the little cubs a stroke. "They *are* very sweet," he said, smiling. "What a day! I suppose Christmas isn't so bad after all," he added quietly.

"I think this has to be the best Christmas ever," announced Great-Uncle Horace.

Zoe picked Meep up and gave him a hug. "And living at

120

the Rescue Zoo makes me the *luckiest* girl ever!" she whispered. "I wonder what adventures will happen at the zoo next year?"

Meep snuggled into Zoe. He couldn't wait to see what kind of animal would be coming to the Rescue Zoo next!

Read about Zoe's first animal adventure!

The cub blinked nervously at the crowd. He opened his mouth to reveal a row of white baby teeth and gave a squeaky growl. His little paws trembled and he looked very weak and frightened.

"Stand back, please!" Mr. Pinch announced as the visitors pushed forward to get a better look. "Make way for the vet."

Zoe's mom knelt down slowly next to the cub. "There, there, little one. I'm not going to hurt you," she soothed as she examined the lion's eyes, ears, teeth, tummy, and paws. The cub shrank away, snarling as fiercely as he could. Zoe's mom looked up. "You found him just in time, Uncle Horace. It looks like he hasn't eaten in weeks."

Zoe and Meep shared a worried look. The cub seemed confused and very scared. He kept turning his head from side to side, as if he was looking for someone in the crowd. Zoe desperately wanted to explain that everyone at the Rescue Zoo was really kind and wanted to help him. But she couldn't talk to him in front of the crowd — she had to keep the animals' secret.

Zoe felt a gentle tug on her hair, and realized it was Kiki trying to get her attention.

Great-Uncle Horace was standing next to her. Leaning closer, he whispered, "My dear, this little chap needs help. Will you promise to look after him for me?"

Zoe stared at her great-uncle and then nodded. "I promise. I'll try my very best to help the cub."